D0575213

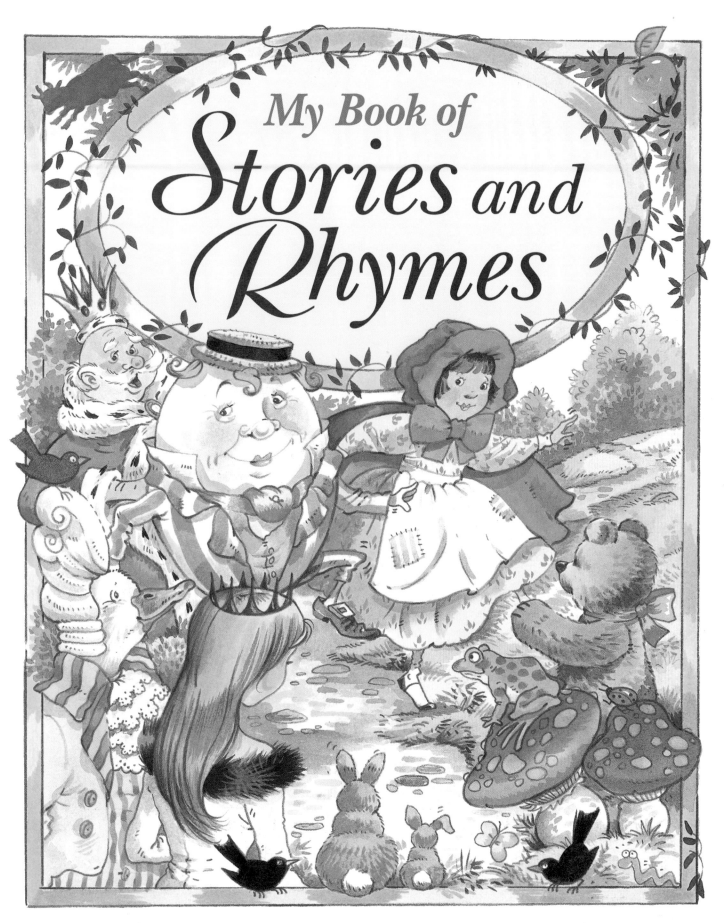

My Book of
Stories and Rhymes

Illustrated by Pamela Storey
Fairy Tales re-written by Maureen Spurgeon
Teddy Stories and Teddy Rhymes by Maureen Spurgeon

Brown Watson
ENGLAND

SING A SONG OF SIXPENCE

Sing a song of sixpence,
A pocket full of rye;
Four and twenty blackbirds
Baked in a pie.

When the pie was opened,
The birds began to sing;
Wasn't that a dainty dish
To set before the King.

The King was in his counting-house,
Counting out his money;
The Queen was in the parlour,
Eating bread and honey.

The maid was in the garden,
Hanging out the clothes,
When down came a blackbird
And pecked off her nose.

They sent for the King's doctor,
Who sewed it on again,
And he sewed it on so neatly,
The seam was never seen.

GOOSEY GANDER

Goosey, goosey gander,
Where do you wander?
Upstairs and downstairs,
And in my lady's chamber,
Where I met an old man,
Who wouldn't say his prayers–
I took him by the left leg,
And threw him down the stairs.

GEORGIE PORGIE

Georgie Porgie, pudding and pie,
Kissed the girls and made them cry;
When the boys came out to play,
Georgie Porgie ran away.

ROCK-A-BYE BABY

Rock-a-bye baby,
On a tree-top,
When the wind blows
The cradle will rock.

When the bough breaks,
The cradle will fall –
Down will come baby,
Cradle and all!

TOM THE PIPER'S SON

Tom, Tom, the piper's son,
Stole a pig and away did run;
The pig was eat,
And Tom was beat,
And Tom went howling down the street.

Teddy's Favourites

What does a Teddy Bear like best?
Perhaps you'd like to know!
Well . . . swings and whirly roundabouts
And a bouncy ball to throw . . .

Currant buns and chocolate,
Honey spread on bread,
And listening to a story,
When I'm tucked up in bed.

Sandcastles! Iced lollipops!
A friendly dog or cat!
Listening to the rain outside
As it goes pitter-pat . . .

Fireside chats when winter comes . . .
A gift from Santa Claus . . .
I think that's all my favourite things.
Can you tell me some of yours?

Teddy's Birthday Party

It was the day of Aunt Bertha Bear's birthday,
and everyone was very busy getting
things ready for a special birthday party.
There were cakes and jellies,
ice creams, sweets, pies, rolls, crisps
and banana boats . . . no wonder Teddy Bear
and his friends could hardly wait for the
fun to begin!

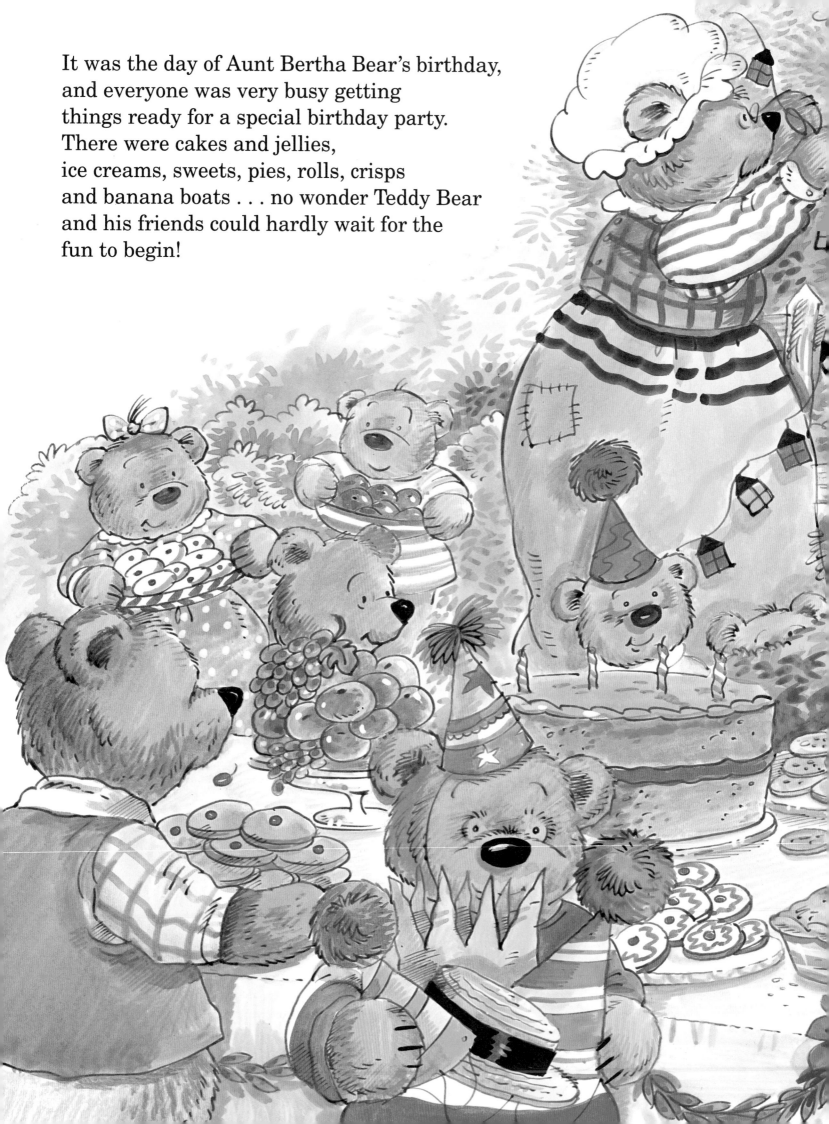

"We'll play lots of jolly games," Aunt Bertha Bear told everyone. "Then Grandfather Bear has promised to bring his Punch and Judy show along!"

That made Teddy Bear smile around at his friends. If there was one thing they enjoyed as much as a birthday party, it was a Punch and Judy Show!

They were halfway through a game of
Musical Chairs before Grandpa Bear
arrived. And he did not seem in a party
mood at all.
"Just look what's happened to poor old
Mr. Punch!" he said, showing them all.
"I got his nose caught in the travelling case,
and I can't possibly mend him in time!"

There was a chorus of disappointed sighs.
"Oh, dear!" said Mummy Bear. "And I suppose Marmaduke is still with Great Uncle Bertram Bear?"
"Yes, indeed," murmured Grandpa. "Ah, my good friend, Marmaduke! If only he were here, now . . ."
"Marmaduke?" echoed Teddy Bear. "Who's Marmaduke?"

"Marmaduke . . ."
Mummy Bear sighed again.
"How he used to make everyone laugh . . ."
"Who's Marmaduke?" Teddy wanted to know. "Always a great favourite . . ." added Grandpa Bear.
"But – who IS Marmaduke?" Teddy asked again, in a much louder voice this time.

11

Grandpa Bear looked at Mummy Bear. She looked at Grandpa. They both looked at Teddy. "Marmaduke?" said Mummy Bear at last. "Everyone likes Marmaduke!" "And I'm sure, Teddy Bear," smiled Grandpa, "that you and your friends will like him, too!" Teddy was very puzzled. Hadn't Mummy said Marmaduke was visiting Great Uncle Bertram?

"Where's Teddy?" asked Barney, as they played Pass the Parcel. "He's missing all the party games!" Before anyone could answer, Mummy Bear clapped her hands. "Please take your seats," she said, "for the birthday show, presented by Grandpa Bear – and Marmaduke!"

"Marmaduke . . ." the whisper went around the room. "Who's Marmaduke?" Aunt Bertha Bear drew the curtains – and who do you think it was? That's right! Teddy Bear, sitting on Grandpa's knee and pretending to be Marmaduke, his dummy!

How the bears laughed at the silly things they did and the funny things Teddy said in the squeaky voice which was really Grandpa's!

THERE WAS AN OLD WOMAN

There was an old woman,
Who lived in a shoe,
She had so many children
She didn't know what to do;
She gave them some broth,
Without any bread,
She whipped them all soundly,
And sent them to bed.

HEY DIDDLE DIDDLE

Hey diddle, diddle
The cat and the fiddle,
The cow jumped over the moon;
The little dog laughed
To see such sport,
And the dish ran away with the spoon.

SLEEPING BEAUTY

Many years ago a King and Queen told everyone of the birth of their baby. The fairies in the land brought the baby gifts, but one wicked fairy promised that when the Princess was fifteen years old, she would prick her finger and go to sleep for one hundred years.

On her fifteenth birthday, the Princess took a walk through her castle and found a room where an old woman sat spinning. "Will you show me how to spin?" the Princess asked.

The old woman showed her what to do but when she touched the needle she pricked her finger and fell asleep at once, and so did everyone else in the castle.

Years passed and one day a handsome Prince was riding by the castle and decided to take a look inside. He was surprised to find that everyone was asleep.

Soon he found the Princess and thought how beautiful she was. He knelt down by her side and kissed her.

At that moment the spell was broken and the Princess and all the other people in the castle woke up from their deep sleep.

The Princess told the Prince
the story of the wicked
fairy's spell and how she
had pricked her finger.

Soon the Prince and the
Princess fell in love with each
other and decided to marry.

The King and Queen arranged a lovely wedding for their daughter and her Prince and all the townsfolk and servants in the castle danced and danced until the next morning.

The Prince and Princess and everyone in the castle lived happily ever after.

23

Teddy's

A B C

"Come with me
And you shall see,
How to learn
Your **a b c**!
Meet my friends!
My family, too!
Each one of them
Will soon help you!
You'll find it's as easy
As it can be,
With us, to learn
Your **a b c**!"

Aa

"Here I am, at my school –
We have lessons every day.
Is there something on my desk
Which begins with a letter **a**?
That's right! It's an **a**pple!
But, that isn't all –
Just look at the posters
Teacher's put on the wall!
There's an **a**nt, **a**lligator –
And an **a**rk, by the way . . .
An **a**crobat . . . what else
Begins with an **a**?"

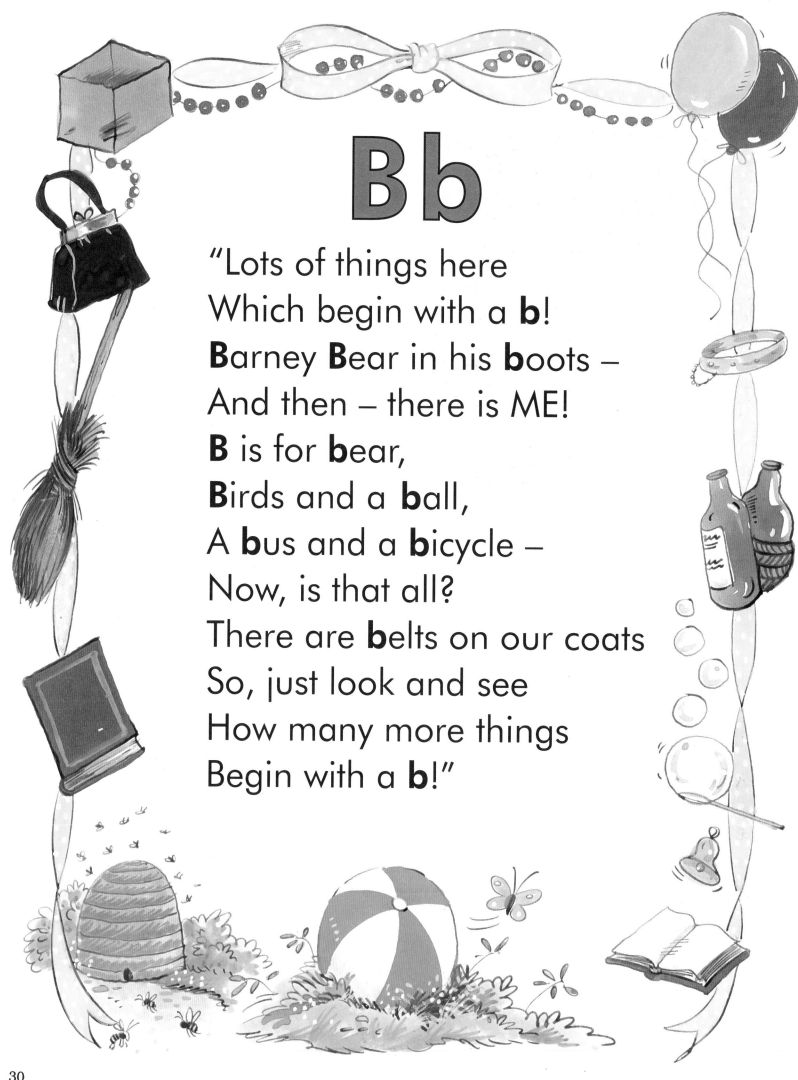

Bb

"Lots of things here
Which begin with a **b**!
Barney **B**ear in his **b**oots –
And then – there is ME!
B is for **b**ear,
Birds and a **b**all,
A **b**us and a **b**icycle –
Now, is that all?
There are **b**elts on our coats
So, just look and see
How many more things
Begin with a **b**!"

Cc

"Picnic time, now!
And the next letter's **c**.
There are **c**ups for our drinks
And our **c**at – can you see?
We eat **c**arrots and **c**ake
And ripe **ch**erries, too!
And **ch**ocolate! Delicious!
Now, let me tell you –
Ch may be
Rather different a sound –
But the first letter's **c**.
Any more to be found?"

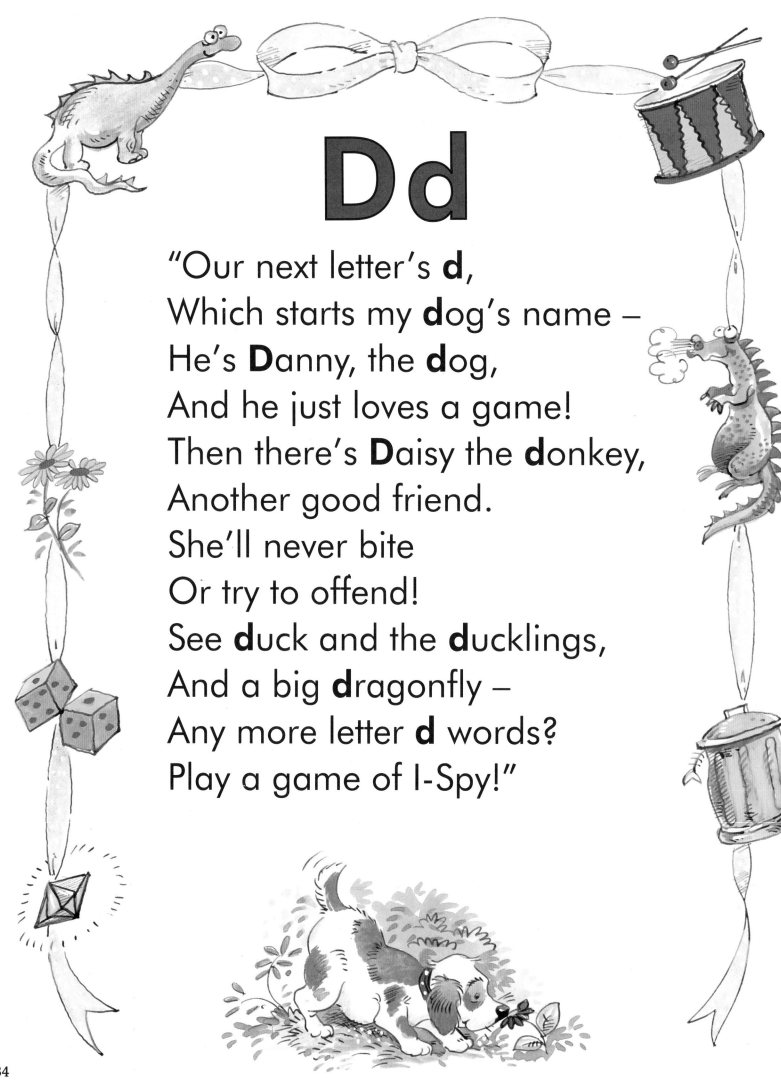

Dd

"Our next letter's **d**,
Which starts my **d**og's name –
He's **D**anny, the **d**og,
And he just loves a game!
Then there's **D**aisy the **d**onkey,
Another good friend.
She'll never bite
Or try to offend!
See **d**uck and the **d**ucklings,
And a big **d**ragonfly –
Any more letter **d** words?
Play a game of I-Spy!"

Ee Ff Gg Hh

"**E** is for **e**ggs,
For a breakfast-time dish.
F is for **f**lowers,
A **f**rog and some **f**ish!
And **f** is for **f**arm
Where my **G**randma, I see!
Her name, of course,
Begins with a **G** . . .
H is for **h**ens,
And a **h**orse eating **h**ay,
And a big **h**elicopter,
Flying swiftly away!"

Ii Jj Kk

"**I** is for **i**ce-cream –
My favourite treat!
Jack-in-the-Box
Would love some to eat!
His name, you know,
Begins with a **J** –
And a big **j**ug of **j**uice
Begins the same way!
Then there's **k** for **k**oala,
My **k**ite and a **k**ing,
And a **k**itten which makes
Knots in the **k**nitting!"

Ll

"**L** is for **l**aces –
One of mine is undone!
A strong **l**ead for Danny –
Every dog should have one.
There are **l**eaves on the trees
And **l**ettuce for tea,
A bright **l**adybird, and
A **l**ollipop for me!
Then a **l**adder for Daddy,
And some **l**etters, too,
Brought by the postman –
Any more words for you?"

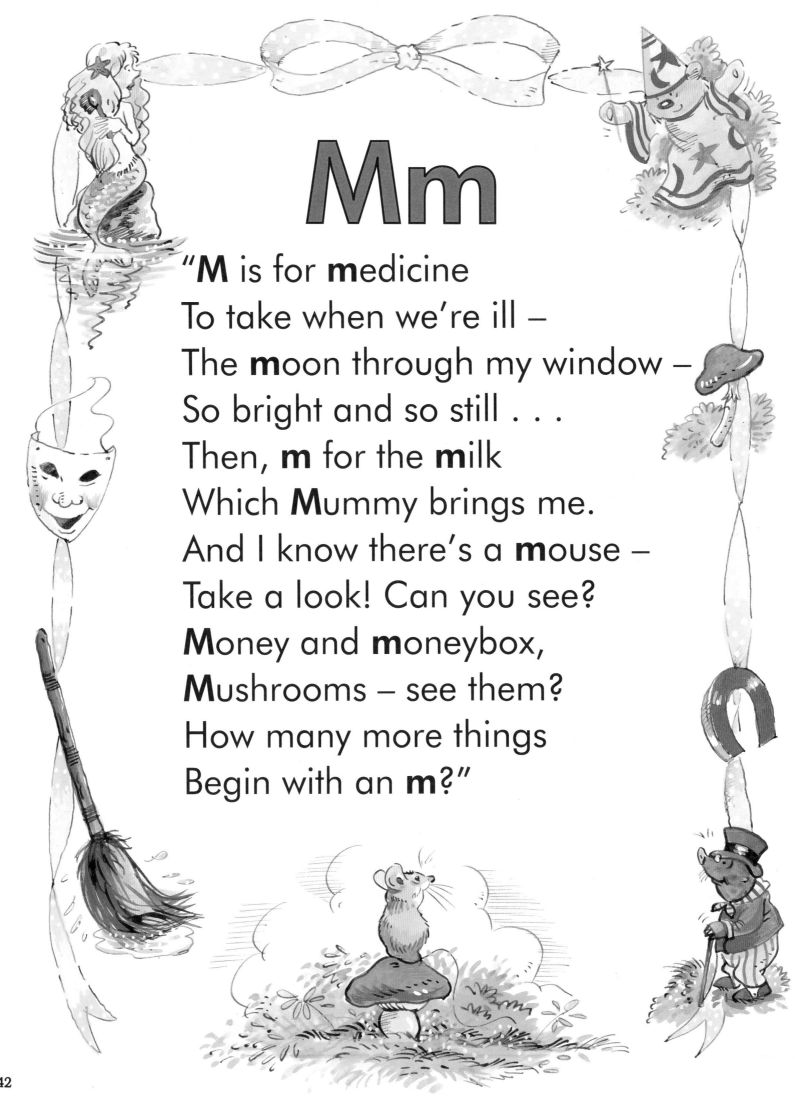

Mm

"**M** is for **m**edicine
To take when we're ill –
The **m**oon through my window –
So bright and so still . . .
Then, **m** for the **m**ilk
Which **M**ummy brings me.
And I know there's a **m**ouse –
Take a look! Can you see?
Money and **m**oneybox,
Mushrooms – see them?
How many more things
Begin with an **m**?"

Nn Oo Pp

"Now we are out camping!
Can you see a **n**est!
A **n**ewspaper for Daddy –
That's what he likes best.
Nest and **n**ewspaper
Both begin with an **n** –
There are **n**uts and a **n**et,
What's the next letter, then?
It's **o** for an **o**wl!
And next comes a **p**,
Which begins **p**ath and **p**illows –
Any more? Look and see!"

Qq Rr Ss

"The next letter is **q**
Which begins the word **q**ueen –
Though, here in our park,
There's not one to be seen!
The **r**ain and the **r**abbits
Begin with – can you guess?
That's right! It's an **r**!
And the next letter's **s**
We have **s** for **s**ee-**s**aw,
A **s**lide and some **s**wings!
Look hard! You may notice
Quite a few other things!"

Tt Uu

"Now, the next letter
Is special to me.
Can you think just why?
It is letter **t**!
Yes! **T** for **T**eddy –
Television, too!
The **t**rack and a **t**unnel . . .
Now, the next letter's **u**
Which begins **u**mbrella
To help keep us dry,
When rain begins falling
From clouds in the sky."

Vv Ww

"**V** for the **v**iolin
Which my Daddy plays.
He's a fine **v**iolinist
Doing practice most days.
There's **v**olcano and **v**ase –
Both begin with a **v** –
W comes next –
Through the **w**indow, you'll see
The **w**ell, with the **w**ater
Which is for us all.
Then Daddy's **w**heelbarrow,
Which he's left by the **w**all!"

Xx Yy Zz

"Now, **x** for the **x**ylophone
I'd like to play!
I had one, you see,
For my birthday, today!
Letter **x** often ends words –
Like si**x**, fi**x** and fo**x** . . .
Then, **y** for my **y**acht –
It was packed in a bo**x**!
Tomorrow, I'm taking it
Out for a sail!
Then **z** is for **z**ebra,
With stripes to his tail!"

Aa

Bb

Cc

Dd

Ee

Ff

Gg

Hh

Ii

Jj

Kk

Ll

Mm

Nn

Oo

Pp

Qq

Rr

Ss

Tt

Uu

Vv

Ww

Xx

Yy

Zz

"Time to go!
But, now you see
How you can learn
Your **a b c**!
And if you'd like
Our help again,
Just turn the pages,
Look – and then,
You'll find it easy
As can be,
To learn, with us,
Your **a b c**!"

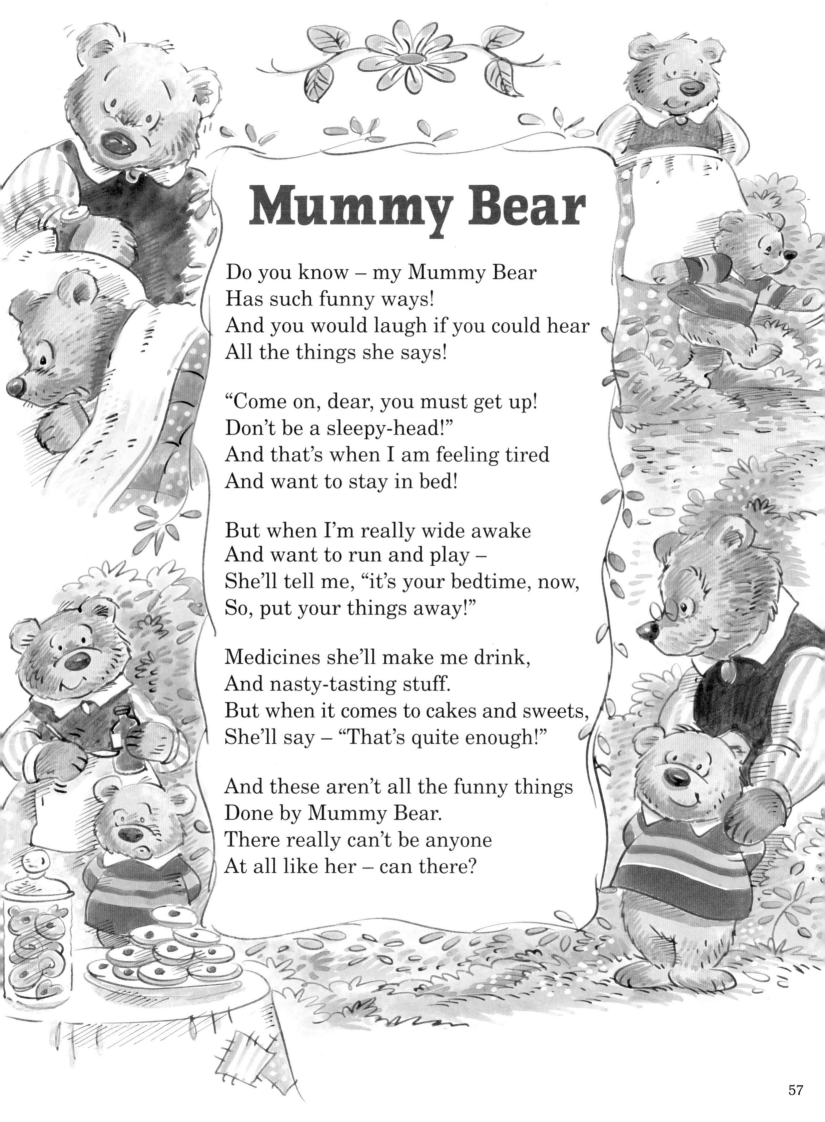

Mummy Bear

Do you know – my Mummy Bear
Has such funny ways!
And you would laugh if you could hear
All the things she says!

"Come on, dear, you must get up!
Don't be a sleepy-head!"
And that's when I am feeling tired
And want to stay in bed!

But when I'm really wide awake
And want to run and play –
She'll tell me, "it's your bedtime, now,
So, put your things away!"

Medicines she'll make me drink,
And nasty-tasting stuff.
But when it comes to cakes and sweets,
She'll say – "That's quite enough!"

And these aren't all the funny things
Done by Mummy Bear.
There really can't be anyone
At all like her – can there?

BYE, BABY BUNTING

Bye, Baby Bunting,
Daddy's gone a-hunting,
Gone to get a rabbit skin
To wrap the Baby Bunting in.

HICKORY, DICKORY DOCK

Hickory, dickory dock,
The mouse ran up the clock.
The clock struck one,
The mouse ran down,
Hickory, dickory dock.

LITTLE MISS MUFFET

Little Miss Muffet
Sat on a tuffet,
Eating her curds and whey;
There came a big spider,
Who sat down beside her
And frightened Miss Muffet away.

TOMMY TUCKER

Little Tommy Tucker sang for his supper;
What shall we give him?
White bread and butter.
How shall he cut it without any knife?
How will he marry, without any wife?

RING-A-RING O' ROSES

Ring-a-ring o' roses,
A pocket full of posies,
A-tishoo! A-tishoo!
We all fall down.

Teddy Goes Flying

One morning, Teddy Bear was looking out of
the window for quite a long time.
"What are you looking at, Teddy?" asked
Mummy Bear at last.
"I'm watching the birds," Teddy Bear told her.
He gave a little sigh. "Oh, Mummy!
It must be lovely to fly around wherever
you want to go, just like them!
Do you think I could learn?"

"Birds have lovely, feathery wings," she said.
"So they're the ones who fly! But we can do lots
of other things, can't we?" Teddy did not
answer. Then he saw something moving along
the window sill. It was a ladybird! Teddy loved
to see these pretty little creatures. He held out
his paw.

Teddy began to say the nursery rhyme which Mummy Bear had taught him. "Ladybird, ladybird . . ." Teddy Bear stopped. Then, he thought hard. Then, he blew very gently on his paw. The ladybird spread her little wings and flew out of the window. Yet, Mummy Bear hadn't said anything at all about beetles being able to fly!

Teddy Bear wandered outside,
where butterflies were flitting among
the flowers! "More things that can fly!"
he thought. Then he heard two bears
calling to each other. "See it fly!"
"Look, up it goes! It's flying!"
It was a beautiful kite sailing up
towards the sky and trailing a bright
paper tail behind it.
"Of course!" cried Teddy. "Kites fly, too!"
He remembered something else.

Kites were like teddy bears. They did not have any wings, either. Just then, an aeroplane streaked across the sky, the sun glinting on its wings – wings which were nothing like the light, feathery wings of the birds. So, how did they fly? After a bit more thinking, Teddy made up his mind to try to fly himself.

But he did not know how to start. He tried jumping, both feet together and flapping his arms about like wings. Then he tried hopping, first on one leg, then on the other. It was quite fun! But Teddy had to stop because he felt so hot and out of breath.

"Maybe," he thought, "if I was up a bit higher, then jumped and flapped my arms, I might fly!" So off he went to Honeypot Hill, climbing up and up to the top. It seemed much higher than it did from his bedroom window. But nothing was going to stop Teddy, now! He shut his eyes tight, made a little run, held his breath – and jumped!

He forgot all about flapping his arms. SPLAT! Teddy landed – splash! – right in the muddy stream at the bottom! "Mummy!" he shouted, feeling all sticky and squelchy and gooey! "Daddy!"

"Teddy!" boomed a voice. "What are you doing down there?" It was Teddy's Uncle Sailor Bill, out flying in the navy helicopter.

Muddy and wet, Teddy Bear was soon hauled up on a rope, higher and higher, towards the helicopter. "I only wanted to fly!" he told his uncle. "Well," laughed Uncle Bill, "you got your wish!"

"Yes," said Teddy, "but the birds, the butterflies, the ladybird and the kite made it look so easy!" He had already decided that flying back to Bear Cottage in a helicopter was exciting enough!

JACK AND JILL

Jack and Jill went up the hill,
To fetch a pail of water;
Jack fell down, and broke his crown,
And Jill came tumbling after.

DIDDLE, DIDDLE, DUMPLING

Diddle, diddle, dumpling, my son John,
Went to bed with his trousers on;
One shoe off and one shoe on,
Diddle, diddle, dumpling, my son John.

LITTLE BOY BLUE

Little Boy Blue,
Come blow your horn;
The sheep's in the meadow,
The cow's in the corn.

Where is the boy
Who looks after the sheep?
He's under the haystack,
Fast asleep.

OLD MOTHER HUBBARD

Old Mother Hubbard
Went to the cupboard,
To get her poor doggy a bone;
But when she got there,
The cupboard was bare,
And so the poor doggy got none!

69

THREE BLIND MICE

Three blind mice, three blind mice,
See how they run, see how they run!
They all ran after the farmer's wife,
Who cut off their tails with the carving knife,
Did you ever see such a thing in your life,
As three blind mice?

SNOW WHITE
and the seven dwarfs

Once upon a time there was a little princess whose skin was so fair that they called her Snow White. She had a stepmother who every day asked her mirror, "Mirror, mirror on the wall, who is the fairest of them all?"

The mirror had always told the Queen that she was the fairest, until one day it said that Snow White was fairer. The Queen was so angry that she told a servant to take Snow White to the woods and kill her.

The servant could not bring himself to kill Snow White but set her free to wander in the woods. Soon she found a tiny cottage where seven little dwarfs lived.

When they arrived home from their work that day, Snow White asked them if she could stay with them and they agreed.

The next day the Queen asked the mirror the usual question but to her horror the mirror replied, "Queen, thou art beauty rare, but Snow White living in the glen with seven little men is many times more beautiful!"

The Queen was very angry and, dressed as an old woman, she went and tried to sell Snow White a petticoat ribbon which would have squeezed her to death, but Snow White refused.

Later that day the Queen visited the cottage again and gave Snow White a rosy apple. Snow White took one bite and fell to the ground poisoned.

One day a Prince arrived in the forest and took Snow White from the glass case in which she lay. The piece of poisoned apple fell from her throat and she awoke. The Queen died shortly after and Snow White and the Prince lived happily ever after.

LITTLE BO-PEEP

Little Bo-peep has lost her sheep,
And doesn't know where to find them;
Leave them alone, and they'll come home,
Bringing their tails behind them.

JACK BE NIMBLE

Jack be nimble,
Jack be quick,
Jack jump over
The candlestick.

WHAT ARE LITTLE GIRLS MADE OF?

What are little girls made of, made of?
What are little girls made of?
Sugar and spice,
And all things nice,
That's what little girls are made of.

What are little boys made of, made of?
What are little boys made of?
Snips and snails,
And puppy dogs' tails,
That's what little boys
are made of.

COCK-A-DOODLE DOO!

Cock-a-doodle doo!
My dame has lost her shoe,
My master's lost his fiddling stick,
And knows not what to do.

Teddy Bear's Surprise

Teddy Bear was feeling so bored! Mummy Bear was busy in the kitchen, Daddy had gone to the market, and there did not seem much to do.

"I've done all my jigsaws!" he told Mummy Bear.
"And I've tidied the toy cupboard!"
"What about digging in the garden?" smiled Mummy.
"Plant some vegetables if you like."
"All right," sighed Teddy. He was not really in the mood for gardening.
"I'll go and ask Barney Bear to help."

"Cheer up, Teddy!" Mummy smiled again.
"You might have a nice surprise before long!"
But Teddy did not think so. And when he found Barney Bear was not at home, he was not at all pleased.
Of course, Teddy should have gone straight back home. Instead, he just marched away.

He didn't look where he was going and
didn't care that he might get lost! Soon,
instead of being bored and angry,
Teddy Bear felt so sad and lonely that
he might have begun to cry – except,
just at that very moment, he heard
somebody laughing . . .

"That's right, ship-mates!" boomed a loud, jolly voice Teddy knew well. "Just enjoy yourselves!" "Uncle Sailor Bill!" cried Teddy, running as fast as he could to where all the laughing and chatter was coming from. "Uncle Sailor Bill, it's me! Teddy Bear!" "Well, scupper me scallywags!" laughed Uncle Bill.

"Come and meet my friends, Teddy!"

Well, there was Posy and Primrose, the twins, Billy Bear and Bobby Bear, Susie, Bella, Tom and Timmy, and lots more bears, all talking and laughing and feeling very excited. "We're going on a treasure hunt!" cried Posy. "There's a picnic first!" said Primrose. "It's a lovely place where we're going, Teddy."

"Do you think Mummy will mind if I come?" Teddy asked. "I think she'll find out soon enough!" laughed Uncle Sailor Bill. Teddy was so pleased! All along the way, Bobby told him about the games of hide-and-seek they would have. "Wait until you see all the hidey-holes, Teddy!" he said. "And the squirrels, and the trees we can climb!"

"And the rounders field!" added Bella. Teddy began to wonder where this exciting place could possibly be. And every time he tried asking about it, Uncle Sailor Bill was busy, either lifting little bears over stiles or making sure nobody was getting left behind. "You'll find out soon enough, Teddy!" was all he would say!

Once or twice, Teddy thought he knew where he was. The clock tower through the trees looked rather like the one in the market near his home, and there was a water fountain he thought he had seen before . . .

"Nearly there, Teddy!" laughed Bobby Bear! "Race you through the trees!" "Don't want to miss the picnic!" cried Billy. Still laughing, they ran through a tunnel of cool, leafy trees with Teddy Bear chasing after them.

This was better than staying at home with nothing to do, he thought! And he made up his mind to ask Uncle Sailor Bill why they couldn't have fun like this where he lived. Teddy chased Billy and Bobby out into the sunshine – and do you know where he found himself?

Across the path from his own front garden!
"You said we were going to this lovely place,"
he told Posy, "with hidey-holes and squirrels
and trees to climb and fields to play in . . ."
"That's right, Teddy!" cried Bobby, swinging
from a tree. "Now, we'll have some fun!"
Just then, out came Mummy Bear with lots
of lovely things for the picnic!

"I see you've met your new friends, Teddy!" she
smiled. "Didn't I say you'd be getting a nice
surprise?"
"Yes," said Teddy, "you did." And he looked
around at the duck pond, and the swing
and the wishing well . . . all the places he loved.
"But coming home was the best surprise of all!"

RIDE A COCK-HORSE TO BANBURY CROSS

Ride a cock-horse to Banbury Cross,
To see a fine lady upon a white horse;
Rings on her fingers and bells on her toes,
She shall have music wherever she goes.

RED RIDING HOOD

One morning Little Red Riding
Hood's mother asked her to take a
basket of food to her Grandma who
was in bed and not feeling very
well. "Do go straight to Grandma's
house," said her mother and
dressed her in her red cape and
hood.

On her way through the wood, Little Red Riding Hood met a wolf who asked her where she was going. "To see my Grandma who is ill in bed," said Little Red Riding Hood.

"Where does she live?" asked the wolf. "At the cottage in the wood," said Little Red Riding Hood without thinking, and before she knew what had happened the wolf turned and ran off.

The wolf rushed straight to the cottage where Grandma lived and when he arrived he knocked at the door. "Who is there?" called Grandma, and the wolf replied, "It's Little Red Riding Hood, Grandma." "Lift the latch and come in," said Grandma. When she saw the wolf she was so frightened, she hid herself in the cupboard.

The wolf quickly put on Grandma's bed-cap and waited for Little Red Riding Hood to arrive. "Who is there?" he called in a voice like Grandma's when he heard her knock. "It is Little Red Riding Hood," she answered. "Lift the latch and come in," said the wolf.

"How are you feeling?" said Little Red Riding Hood. "Much better thank you dear," said the wolf and as he spoke, his bed-cap slipped from his head so that Little Red Riding Hood could see his ears. "What big ears you have!" said Little Red Riding Hood nervously. "All the better to hear you with," said the wolf.

"What big teeth you have," cried Little Red Riding Hood. "All the better to eat you with," shouted the wolf as he jumped out of the bed. "You are not my Grandma!" screamed Little Red Riding Hood. "No, I am the big bad wolf, and I am going to eat you up!"

As Little Red Riding Hood ran from the house, a woodcutter who was cutting some trees outside heard her cries for help. He chased the wolf down the path and the wolf ran off into the woods as fast as he could.

The woodcutter took Little Red Riding Hood back into the cottage to see if the nasty wolf had eaten her Grandma. As they called her, a voice said, "I am in the cupboard, is it safe to come out?" When Grandma heard Little Red Riding Hood's voice she knew that all was well.

"How lucky we both are to be safe!" said Little Red Riding Hood as she hugged her Grandma.

They both thanked the woodcutter and asked him to stay for tea.

Teddy's

Can you count to ten?
It's easy to do!
Mummy Bear showed me –
So I know that it's true!
Will you help with my party
And count things with me?
We'll have lots of fun
Together – you'll see!
And when it's all ready,
You'll be saying by then –
"It really is easy
To count up to ten!"

1 one

"It's my birthday, today!"
Teddy cries out with glee.
"And lots of my friends
Are coming to tea!"
"But," says his Mummy,
"I need your help, too!
There's lots of counting
I want you to do!"
"One birthday cake!"
Mummy Bear thinks.
One is such a nice number,
But what can we drink?

2 two

"Here's your drink, Teddy!"
Mummy says with a smile,
"There's enough here to last
Your friends quite a while!
Two big jugs of cool lemonade!
Lots more in the kitchen!
It's all freshly made!"
"One cake, two jugs!
One, two!" Teddy cries.
"What's next to be counted?
Another surprise?"

2 =

3 three

When they go back inside,
Mummy Bear piles up high
Three dishes with crisps!
Teddy gives a glad cry.
"One, two, three dishes!"
Mummy says, "Yes, that's right!
Take them into the garden!
No taking a bite!"
"So, one birthday cake,
And two jugs! One, two!
And three dishes!" says Teddy.
"Now, what shall I do?"

3 =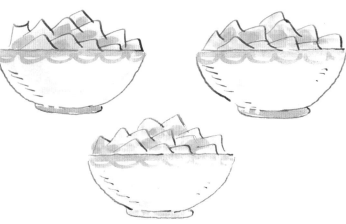

4 four

"Birthday candles!" smiles Mummy.
"We need three and one more . . ."
Teddy shouts out, "I know!
That's one, two, three, four!
Four candles, Mummy!
And I'm four, today!"
And he hands them to her,
To go on display!
They look nice on the cake –
He's as pleased as can be!
What's the next number?
Teddy can't wait to see!

4 =

5 five

One, two, three, four –
Five plates of cheese!
Mummy says, "Try a piece!"
Teddy answers, "Yes, please!"
At once, he decides
It's delicious to eat –
A tasty surprise,
And a savoury treat!
Outside, comes a cry –
"We've arrived, Teddy Bear!"
And Mummy Bear smiles,
"Your next number's there!"

5 =

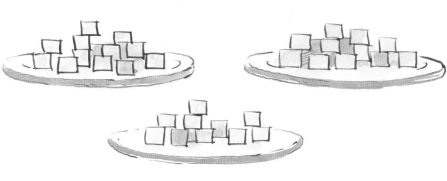

6 six

As Mummy Bear speaks,
The garden gate clicks . . .
"My friends!" shouts out Teddy.
"There ought to be six!
One, two, three, four,
Five, six!" Teddy grins.
"Here, have a balloon!
Now, my party begins!"
"Well, count the balloons!"
Mummy says. "One, two, three."
"Four, five, six!" joins in Teddy,
As pleased as can be!

6 =

7 seven

"Inside, for a moment!"
Calls Mummy Bear.
"Each of you will need
To take out a chair!
Teddy, six for your friends,
Then one for you!
So, there should be seven!"
He sees if that's true . . .
"One, two, three, four,
Five, six, seven chairs!
We've got one chair each!
What's next for us bears?"

7 =

8 eight

"Party hats!" smiles Mummy,
And in through the gate,
Comes Teddy's own Daddy,
He hopes he's not late.
"Now for the party hats,
Let's try them for size.
Yours doesn't count, Mummy!"
Teddy Bear cries,
"One, two, three, four, five,
Six, seven, eight!
Now let's have some lemonade,
Before it's too late!"

8 =

9 nine

"Teddy," smiles Mummy,
"We shall each need a straw –
That's eight straws for us,
Then, for Daddy, one more!"
Teddy Bear counts them out –
He's doing just fine!
"One, two, three, four, five,
Six, seven, eight, nine!
Nine straws, Mummy Bear,
To go in our drinks!"
"Now, what's the next number?"
Teddy Bear thinks . . .

9 =

10 ten

"Each friend's brought a present,
So I know that is six . . ."
Teddy would hate
To get into a fix . . .
"Then – two presents from Mummy,
From Daddy, two more . . .
So, if I am right,
That should make it four . . .
So, that's six, add on four . . ."
Teddy counts up again.
"One, two, three, four, five, six,
Seven, eight, nine, ten!"

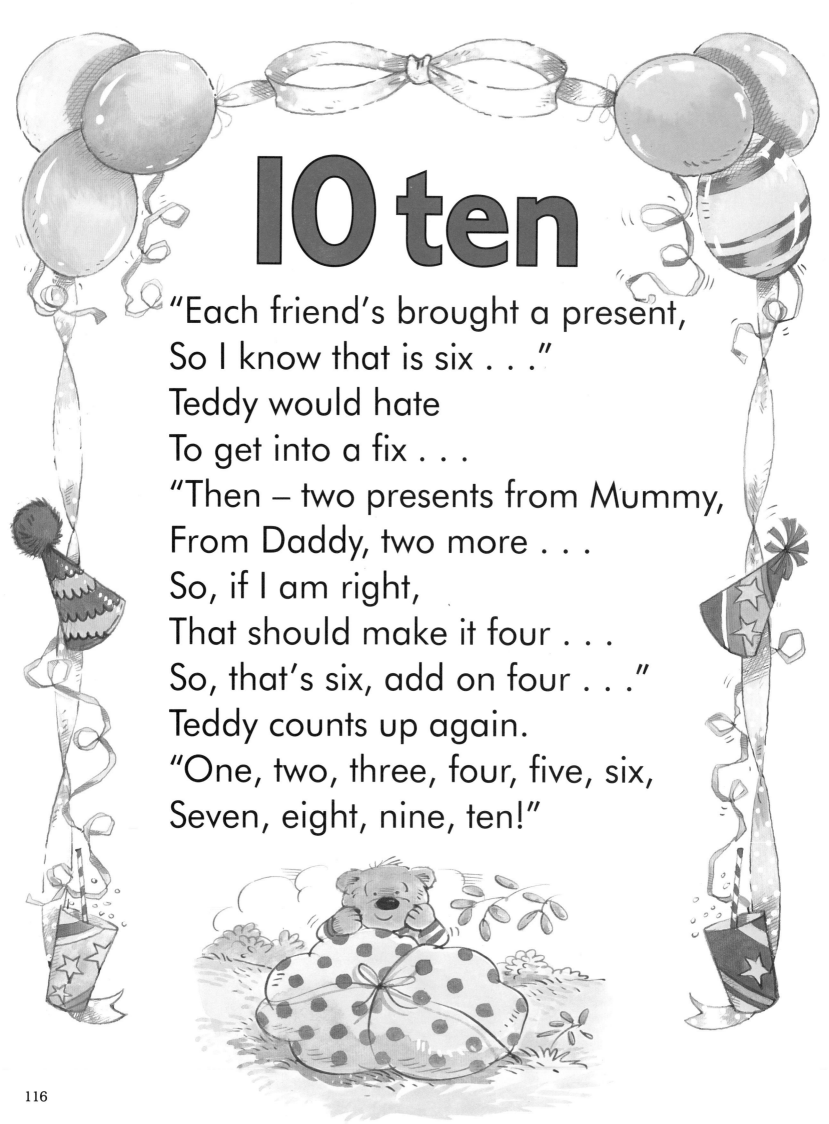

10 =

There's a kite! And a ball!
A car and a train!
A boat and a drum
And a little toy plane,
A puppet, some pencils –
A bicycle, too!
Then everyone sings,
"Happy Birthday to you!"
"Oh, thank you!" cries Teddy.
And he counts up again.
"One, two, three, four, five,
Six, seven, eight, nine, ten!"

"So, that's one birthday cake,
Two jugs, lemonade,
Three dishes of crisps,
Four candles displayed!
Five plates of cheese,
With six friends to share!
That's seven little teddies –
Each one needs a chair!
Eight party hats –
And nine straws for drinks,
Then comes ten presents –
That's great!" Teddy thinks.

Now, his friends have all gone,
Teddy gets into bed,
Looking round at his cards –
A real sleepyhead!
"Today, I was four,
I'll be five next year!"
He tells himself, softly,
So that no one can hear.
Then he closes his eyes,
And counts, once again –
But he's fast asleep
Long before number ten!

1

2

3

4

5

6

7

8

9

10

There'll be lots of birthdays
For me – and for you!
But this one was special –
And lots of fun, too!
Now, we can tell,
How to count up to ten.
And if you forget,
You'll remember again,
If you go through my book
And count up the ways
My birthday became
The happiest of days!

HERE WE GO ROUND THE MULBERRY BUSH

Here we go round the mulberry bush,
The mulberry bush, the mulberry bush,
Here we go round the mulberry bush,
On a cold and frosty morning.

CURLY LOCKS

Curly Locks, Curly Locks, will you be mine?
You shall not wash dishes, nor yet feed the swine;
You'll sit on a cushion and sew a fine seam,
And feed upon strawberries, sugar and cream.

PUSSY CAT, PUSSY CAT

Pussy cat, pussy cat,
Where have you been?
I've been up to London,
To visit the Queen.

Pussy cat, pussy cat,
What did you there?
I frightened a little mouse,
'Neath the Queen's chair.

THE CROOKED MAN

There was a crooked man,
And he walked a crooked mile.
He found a crooked sixpence
Beside a crooked stile;

He bought a crooked cat,
Which caught a crooked mouse,
And they all lived together
In a little crooked house.

TO BED, TO BED

"To bed, to bed!" said Sleepy Head.
"Tarry a while," said Slow.
"Put on the pan," said greedy Ann.
"We'll sup before we go."

129

All Year Round

When Spring-time comes, there's lots to do –
Watching birds and squirrels, too.
Flying kites and pressing flowers,
Now there are more daylight hours.

Summer-time! And, to keep cool,
We play in my big paddling pool!
Picnic lunches, games outside –
Scooters, tricycles to ride.

Autumn now, and all around,
Leaves come fluttering to the ground.
Bonfires, conkers to collect,
And the wild birds to protect.

Winter comes with frost and snow,
We think of someone we all know
Coming down a chimney stack . . .
Can you guess what's in his sack?

Teddy's Seaside Adventure

Teddy Bear was enjoying himself at the seaside!
There was so much to do! Best of all,
there was a beach competition, with prizes
for the best sand-castles. The competition was
being judged by Captain Bear – and everyone
was wondering who would win! Captain Bear
had been showing Teddy and his friends how
to build the very best sand-castles –

so, even without any prizes, they'd
already had lots of fun! The only snag
was Bully Bear . . . He was forever
teasing the little bears, spoiling their
sand-castles, running off with their
sweets and burying things in the sand.

"I'd like to give that bear a few things!" growled Captain Bear. "Like a good spanking and no sweets for a fortnight!" "Bully's too strong for any of us!" said Barney Bear, Teddy's friend. "What can we do, Teddy?"

Teddy Bear did not answer. It was very hard to think of a way to beat a big bear like Bully. Later on, Teddy gave Teeny Bear an envelope. "Can you take this to Teacher Bear, Teeny?" he said. "Captain Bear's written down where all the prizes for the sand-castle competition have been hidden, so that Bully Bear doesn't find them!"

"That's what you think, Teddy Bear!" said Bully Bear. He snatched the letter and ran off, laughing.

All that afternoon, Teddy and his friends worked hard on their sand-castles. "Well," said Barney, "at least you got Bully Bear out of the way, Teddy!" He did not say anything about them losing all the prizes for the sand-castle competition – but the bears could not help being disappointed . . .

Suddenly, Captain Bear gave an angry yell. "What do you mean by digging up my sandcastle?" he roared at Bully Bear. "You ruffian!"

"B-but, I-I didn't . . ." faltered Bully Bear. "I thought the prizes were here. I-I mean . . ."

"Thought you'd have them for yourself, did you?" thundered Captain Bear. He almost threw Bully Bear across the beach!

"Go away," he roared, "and don't come back, spoiling things for everyone else!"

"See that, Teddy?" grinned Barney. "Good thing Bully believed the note you wrote about the prizes being buried under Captain's sand-castle!" Clever Teddy Bear!

My Friends

I like it when I'm with my friends,
Having games and playing, too.
But when they've gone, it's rather nice
To have nothing much to do!

LADYBIRD, LADYBIRD

Ladybird, ladybird,
Fly away home,
Your house is on fire
And your children all gone;
All except one,
And that's little Ann,
And she crept under
The warming pan.

COBBLER, COBBLER

Cobbler, cobbler, mend my shoe,
Get it done by half-past-two;
Stitch it up and stitch it down,
Then I'll give you half-a-crown.

MARY, MARY

Mary, Mary, quite contrary,
How does your garden grow?
With silver bells and cockle shells,
And pretty maids all in a row.

LITTLE JACK HORNER

Little Jack Horner sat in the corner,
Eating a Christmas pie;
He put in his thumb,
And pulled out a plum,
And said, "What a good boy am I!"

The Day Has Begun!

Butterflies flitter,
Baby birds twitter.
Caterpillars awake.
Leaves gently shake.
And here comes the sun –
The day has begun!

CINDERELLA

Cinderella lived in a big house with her father and two stepsisters. The stepsisters were very unkind to her and made her do all the housework. Although she was pretty they made her dress in rags instead of nice clothes.

Cinderella's stepsisters spent most of their time in front of the mirror powdering their noses and making Cinderella brush their hair.

One day an invitation to the ball
arrived from the palace.
"May I go?" asked Cinderella.

Cinderella's stepsisters
laughed and said that it was
impossible. This made
Cinderella very sad. When
her stepsisters finally left for
the ball, Cinderella sat
crying by the fire.

143

Cinderella was quite alone in the house, and was surprised to hear a voice saying, "I am your Fairy Godmother, and you shall go to the ball. Bring me a pumpkin, four white mice and three lizards."

As fast as lightning, the pumpkin was changed into a coach, the four white mice into four lovely white horses and the lizards into a coach driver and two footmen.

When the Fairy Godmother waved her wand, Cinderella's rags changed into a wonderful ball dress and she had dainty glass slippers on her feet. "You must leave the palace before twelve o' clock, or everything will change back to how it was before," her Fairy Godmother told her.

145

Cinderella so enjoyed dancing with the Prince that she forgot the time and soon the clock struck twelve. She ran quickly down the palace steps. As she ran, the Prince tried to stop her, but she was gone.

The Prince found one of Cinderella's tiny glass slippers and told his footmen, "I will marry the girl whose foot it will fit!"

The footmen travelled for many miles in search of the owner, and, on their way back to the palace, they called at Cinderella's house. The two stepsisters tried to make the slipper fit them, but it was no use.

Just as they were leaving, Cinderella's father said that she should be allowed to try the slipper. It fitted her perfectly. Cinderella married the Prince and became the happiest girl in the land.

Uncle Sailor Bill

Teddy is so excited today. His Uncle Sailor Bill has promised to take him and all his friends on a special boat trip to Plumtree Island, with a picnic and a sing-song around a camp-fire.

Only Mummy Bear seems worried. She has seen the big storm clouds gathering in the sky . . . .

Suddenly, down comes the rain.

"Quick!" cries Teddy. "Make for the boat-house!"

Poor Teddy! He and his friends have been looking forward to their special treat for so long – and now it looks as if it is all going to be spoilt.

"My Uncle Sailor Bill has sailed half-way round the world!" Teddy tells everyone. "A thunder storm won't stop him from getting here."

He has hardly finished speaking, when – guess who comes into the boat-house, shaking a shower of raindrops from his hat? That's right! It's Uncle Sailor Bill, smiling all over his face.

"Ahoy there, me hearties!" he calls out in his loud voice. "Just the weather for a shipwreck, eh?"

"A shipwreck?" echoes Teddy.

"That's right," smiles Uncle Sailor Bill. "Come on, shipmates! Let's collect up all the things we can use to keep afloat."

Then, do you know what Uncle Sailor Bill does next? He turns every chair upside-down!

"This is going to be the best shipwreck, ever," he keeps saying. "Teddy, see if you can roll up that mat, will you?"

"All right, Uncle," says Teddy.

Nobody quite knows what is happening, but it seems a lot of fun.

By the time they have finished, the boat-house looks such a mess! As well as the upturned chairs, there are planks of wood and empty chests all over the place, rolled-up mats and piles of old sacks . . .

Mummy Bear holds up her paws in horror – but Teddy and his friends are so busy enjoying themselves, they don't even think about the rain pouring down outside.

"Look lively, shipmates!" booms Uncle Sailor Bill. "Time to get all round the wreck without falling into the sea!"

"That means we must try not to step on the floor!" Teddy shouts out. "We don't want to get caught by the pirate king!"

"A pirate king?" Uncle Sailor Bill laughs. "First time I've ever been called that, Teddy!"

When they've all gone round the shipwreck at least twice, Uncle Sailor Bill calls out: "Time for ship's rations!" and throws back the lid of a great, big picnic hamper packed with all sorts of good things to eat and drink.

Then Uncle Sailor Bill takes out his concertina, and everyone is soon joining in with all the jolly songs that they know.

Suddenly, one of the little bears gives a cry.

"Look, everyone! It's stopped raining!"

"So it's a voyage to Plumtree Island, after all," says Uncle Sailor Bill. "Get the boat-house ship-shape, then we set sail."

The boat ride to Plumtree Island is lovely – but because of the rain, Uncle Sailor Bill says it's too wet to land.

"Sorry, shipmates," he says. "Maybe, next time, eh? When it's fair weather for sailing."

Teddy smiles round at his friends. Each of them can't help hoping for another shipwreck the next time they meet his Uncle Sailor Bill!

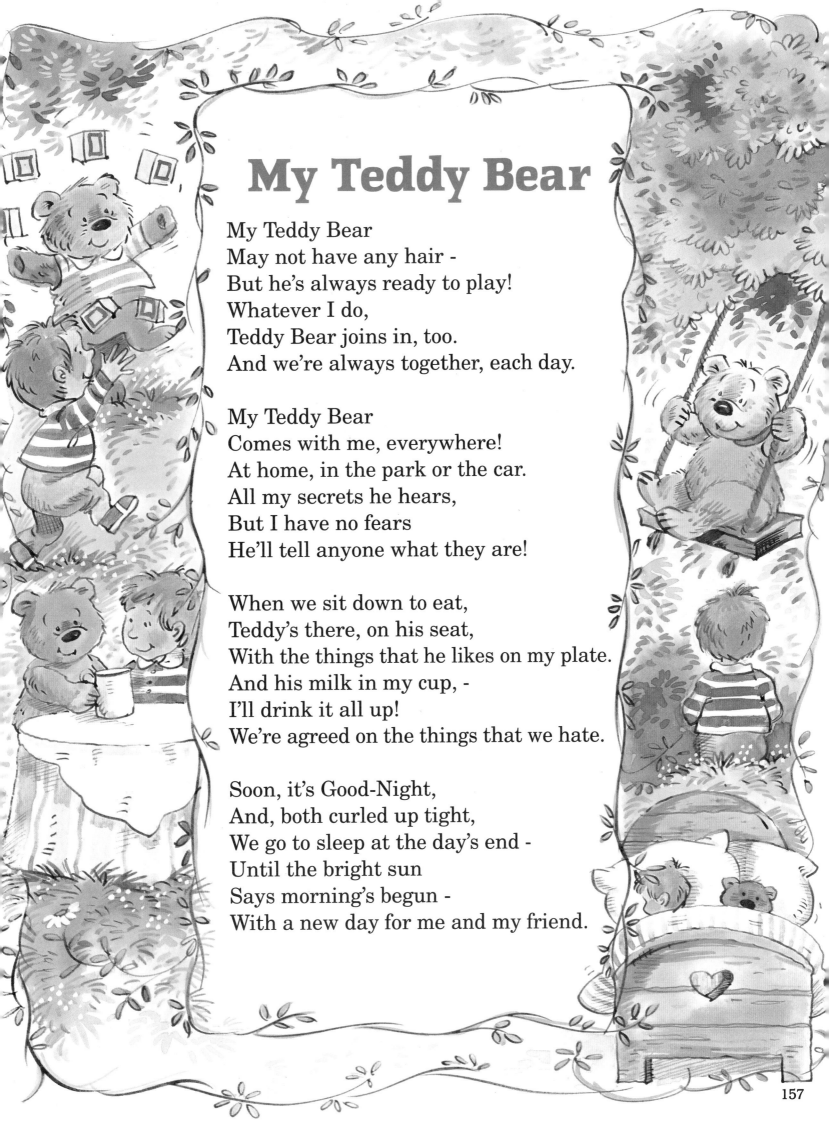

My Teddy Bear

My Teddy Bear
May not have any hair -
But he's always ready to play!
Whatever I do,
Teddy Bear joins in, too.
And we're always together, each day.

My Teddy Bear
Comes with me, everywhere!
At home, in the park or the car.
All my secrets he hears,
But I have no fears
He'll tell anyone what they are!

When we sit down to eat,
Teddy's there, on his seat,
With the things that he likes on my plate.
And his milk in my cup, -
I'll drink it all up!
We're agreed on the things that we hate.

Soon, it's Good-Night,
And, both curled up tight,
We go to sleep at the day's end -
Until the bright sun
Says morning's begun -
With a new day for me and my friend.

JACK SPRAT COULD EAT NO FAT

Jack Sprat could eat no fat,
His wife could eat no lean,
So it came to pass, between them both,
They licked the platter clean.

Jack ate all the lean,
Joan ate all the fat,
The bone they picked it clean,
Then gave it to the cat.

THERE WAS A LITTLE GIRL

There was a little girl and she had a little curl,
Right in the middle of her forehead;
When she was good, she was very, very good,
But when she was bad, she was horrid!

SIMPLE SIMON

Simple Simon met a pieman,
Going to the fair;
Said Simple Simon to the pieman:
"Let me taste your ware."
Said the pieman to Simple Simon:
"Show me first your penny."
Said Simple Simon to the pieman:
"Indeed, I have not any."

POLLY PUT THE KETTLE ON

Polly put the kettle on,
Polly put the kettle on,
Polly put the kettle on,
We'll all have tea.

Sukey take it off again,
Sukey take it off again,
Sukey take it off again,
They've all gone home.

Round and Round the Garden

Round and round the garden,
Like a teddy bear,
One step, Two steps,
Tickle you under there.

Round and round the haystack,
Went the little mouse.
One step, Two steps,
In his little house.

The Doll's House

Teddy Bear always likes calling in to see his friend, the Toymaker. His workshop is such a nice, warm place to be, with lots of interesting things going on.

"Nice to see you, Teddy!" the Toymaker smiled one morning. "Come over to my bench and tell me what you think of this doll's house I'm making for the Children's Hospital."

Teddy, thought how pleased the children would be.

"Isn't it their party tomorrow?" asked Teddy.

"Yes," said the Toymaker.

Next day, Teddy decided to go past the Children's Hospital on his way to the Toymaker's workshop.

Everyone was busy, putting up decorations and setting out the tables ready for the party

"If only the children had something nice to see from their balcony, instead of this ugly, old wall," sighed Matron.

"Even the birds don't stay long because there is nowhere for them to feed!"

Teddy wished he could help.

"Not much fun sitting out on a balcony when there is nothing to see. Never mind!" he told himself. "Just wait until the Toymaker brings the lovely doll's house!" He could hardly wait to see it, himself!

But, as he turned the corner, the Toymaker came hurrying towards him, looking very upset.

"Such a dreadful thing has happened, Teddy!" he cried. "I left my workshop window open last night so that the paint would dry, and the rain came in and made the wood swell. Now the walls don't fit, so I can't put the floors in, either!"

"Oh, dear!" said Teddy. "And you worked so hard!"

Then Teddy had an idea!

"Toymaker," he said, "can you fix some hooks to the bottom of the house, and take out the back wall? Perhaps make the roof a bit thicker, too?"

"Yes," said the Toymaker in surprise, "but . . ."

"Do that, then bring it to the Children's Hospital," said Teddy. "I'll meet you there."

And off Teddy went into the woods with his Daddy.
Together, they collected all the nuts and berries
and pips they could find. Then Mummy Bear
gave them some pieces of stale bread and an old
saucer – and off they all went to meet the
Toymaker at the Children's Hospital.

It really was a very good idea . . .

Soon, the Toymaker was fixing the strange-looking house on to the wall . . . And even before Teddy had put out all the berries, the nuts, the pips, the stale bread and a saucer of water, birds began flying in and out of their new home!

"What a sight for the children to see from the balcony!" cried Matron. "Thank you, Toymaker!"

"And thank you, Teddy!" smiled the Toymaker.

Grumpy Bertie Bear

Near the cottage where Teddy Bear lives with his Mummy and Daddy there are some lovely woods. He and Daddy Bear often go out walking and love to see all the birds and woodland friends.

"We've had a lot of rain lately," said Daddy one morning. "The ground's too wet to go far, Teddy, so I think . . ."

Teddy grabbed his Daddy's arm. "Listen!" he said. "I'm sure I heard a voice!"

"ATISHOO!" someone sneezed. "Oh, dear! Oh, dear! I feel so dreadful! And I ache all over!"

"Sounds like another bear!" cried Daddy, leading the way through the trees.

"Look, just under this clump of bushes."

"Who are you?" asked Teddy Bear kindly.

"The name's Bertie," answered the bear, sneezing again. "Ooh, I'm soaked to the skin!"

"You'd best come home with us," said Daddy Bear. "Take his arm, Teddy."

Before long, Bertie was sitting in Daddy's chair with Teddy's dressing gown on. And as he sipped a nice cup of hot chocolate, he began telling his story.

"I belong to a girl called Lavinia," he said.

He looked all around the cosy, little cottage.

"The house where we live is much bigger than this!" he added. Mummy Bear bit her lip.

"So, how did you come to be left in the woods?" asked Teddy politely.

"Lavinia went off picking flowers," growled Bertie. "I suppose she got caught in the rain and ran straight home. She would never have left me behind on purpose."

"No, of course not," smiled Daddy. "Look, we'll find you some dry clothes, then go back to the woods when you're feeling better, Bertie. Maybe Lavinia will be there looking for you."

Teddy managed to find a pair of trousers and a warm, woolly jumper to fit Bertie – even a pair of smart shoes and socks!

"Try these on for size, Bertie," he smiled.

Bertie Bear did not seem very pleased.

"Not really my colour," he said, fingering the jersey. "And Lavinia threw out a pair of trousers much better than these!" He gave a deep sigh. "Still, I suppose they are better than nothing. I'll get a whole set of new clothes once I'm back home, anyway."

"What a nasty, old bear," thought Teddy. "He hasn't even said "Thank You", yet!"

In the end, Mummy, Daddy and Teddy Bear were glad when the time came for Bertie to go back to the woods. Daddy and Teddy waited to see if the little girl would come back to find him. Presently, they heard a voice.

"Lavinia, dear, come here a minute!"

It was a little, old lady, squeezing her way towards the clump of bushes where Bertie sat.

"Lavinia," she smiled, as a little girl appeared, "isn't this the bear you lost the other day?" It was then that Teddy saw the lovely doll which Lavinia held.

"What, that old thing, Auntie?" she cried. "Look at him. Somebody must have thrown him away!"

Bertie looked as if he were about to cry. She went off, leaving the old lady to pick up Bertie Bear.

"Do you know," she said, stroking his head, "you remind me of a Teddy Bear I had when I was a girl, about the same age as my great niece, Lavinia. How would you like to come home with me? I'm sure my grandchildren would love to play with you when they come to tea."

The hurt look on Bertie Bear's face vanished in an instant.

Teddy could see the corners of his mouth turning up into a happy smile, his black eyes shining like new, just to know that he was loved and wanted once again.

"What are you thinking about, Teddy?" asked Daddy.

"I was just wondering," said Teddy, "if Bertie Bear will call at our cottage again."

173

HUMPTY DUMPTY

Humpty Dumpty sat on a wall,
Humpty Dumpty had a great fall;
All the King's horses and all the King's men,
Couldn't put Humpty together again.

A Special Friend

Do you have a special friend
Who's loved by everyone?
Someone who can always make
A dull day seem like fun?

A friend who smiles and waves a hand
And keeps you smiling, too?
A friend who thinks of games to play
And lots of things to do?

And no matter how you're feeling,
You know your friend is there.
Just like someone we ALL know –
Our good friend, TEDDY BEAR!

The Three Bears

Teddy Bear loves honey! Best of all, he likes it spread on hot toast at breakfast-time. So he's a bit disappointed when he sees Mummy Bear making porridge instead.

"Can't I have honey?" he asks,

"Porridge is good for you on cold mornings like this, Teddy," smiles Mummy. "Come and stir the oats with a little milk in my mixing bowl."

Mixing and stirring is usually one of Teddy's favourite jobs – but Daddy Bear notices that he doesn't look too happy about it, today . . .

"Don't worry about eating up your porridge," he smiles, sitting down in his big chair. "Someone might come along and start eating it for you."

Teddy stops stirring at once.

"Someone eating my porridge?" he cries. "I don't believe it!"

"I expect that's what the other three bears thought," says Mummy, pouring the rest of the milk into a saucepan.

"What other bears?" asks Teddy. He forgets about not having honey for breakfast. "Tell me, Mummy!"

"Well," says Mummy, "there was a Daddy Bear, a Mummy Bear and a Baby Bear. They lived in a cottage at the edge of a wood."

"Just like us!" Teddy says.

"Yes, that's right," Mummy nods, stirring busily.

"Well, this Mummy Bear had just made the porridge, but it was too hot. So, they went for a walk in the woods whilst it cooled down. And along came a little girl with such lovely, long, golden curls that she was called Goldilocks. She saw the three bears' cottage, and went inside."

"And did she eat the porridge?" asks Teddy.

"Only Baby Bear's! She tried Daddy Bear's porridge, but that was too hot, and she tried Mummy Bear's porridge, but that was too cold."

"Then what happened?" Teddy wants to hear the rest of the story, so Mummy tells him how Goldilocks sat in Daddy Bear's chair, but that was too hard.

"Then she sat in Mummy Bear's chair, but that was too soft."

"Did she sit in Baby Bear's chair?" asks Teddy.

Mummy nods again. "Yes. But she was so heavy after eating the porridge, she broke it in pieces! By the time the three bears came back, Goldilocks had gone upstairs to have a rest."

Teddy's Mummy has left the porridge on top of the stove to keep it hot. Now, when she pours it into the breakfast dishes, it is too hot to eat!

"Let's go for a walk," says Daddy. "Just down to the edge of the wood and back."

"Good idea!" agrees Mummy. "It's such a lovely, crisp morning. Put your scarf on, Teddy."

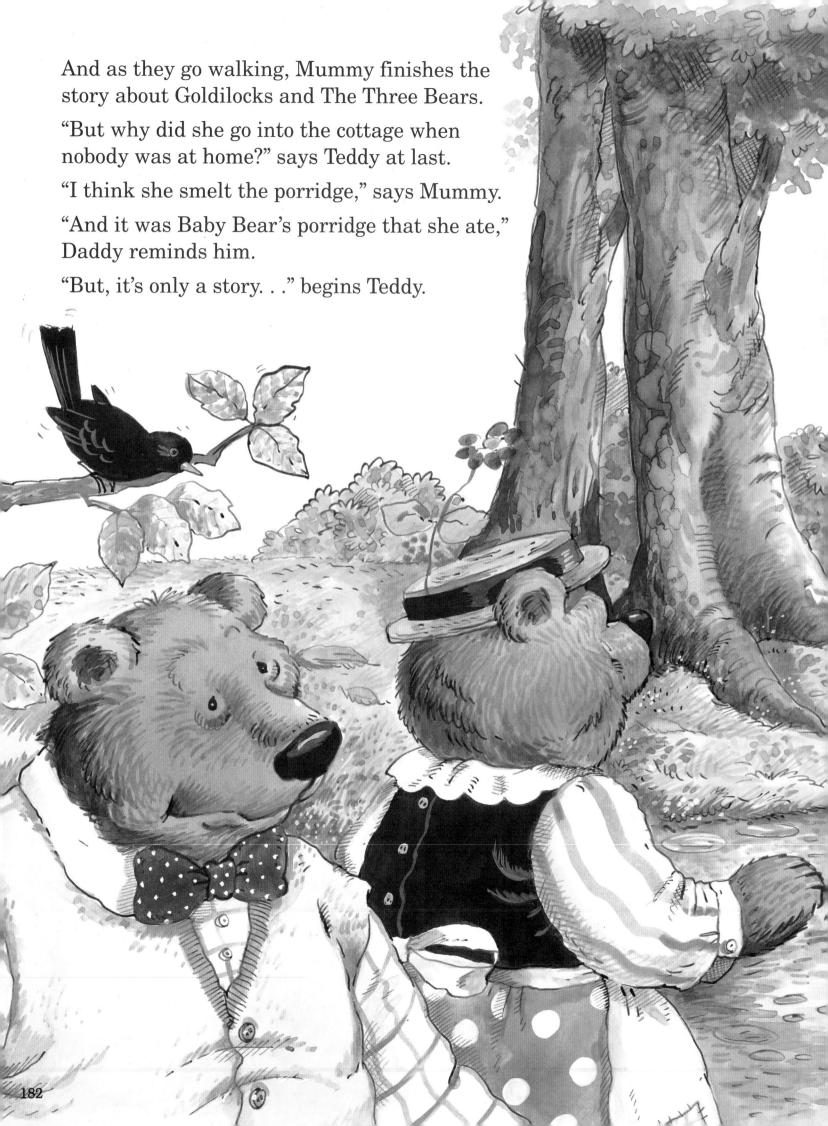

And as they go walking, Mummy finishes the story about Goldilocks and The Three Bears.

"But why did she go into the cottage when nobody was at home?" says Teddy at last.

"I think she smelt the porridge," says Mummy.

"And it was Baby Bear's porridge that she ate," Daddy reminds him.

"But, it's only a story. . ." begins Teddy.

Then, he stops. He is sure he has just seen someone going towards the little cottage at the edge of the wood . . . someone with long, golden curls bobbing about in the breeze . . .

"Come on!" he shouts, and begins to run as fast as he can. "Let's go home!"

He has quite decided that he doesn't want Goldilocks eating up **his** porridge, this morning!

WEE WILLIE WINKIE

Wee Willie Winkie
Runs through the town,
Upstairs and downstairs
In his nightgown;
Rapping at the window,
Crying through the lock,
Are the children all in bed,
For now it's eight o'clock.

POLLY FLINDERS

Little Polly Flinders
Sat among the cinders,
Warming her pretty little toes;
Her mother came and caught her,
And smacked her little daughter,
For spoiling her nice new clothes.

MARY HAD A LITTLE LAMB

Mary had a little lamb,
Its fleece was white as snow,
And everywhere that Mary went
That lamb was sure to go.

It followed her to school one day–
That was against the rule;
It made the children laugh and play,
To see a lamb at school.

SEE-SAW MARGERY DAW

See-saw Margery Daw,
Jack shall have a new master;
Jack shall work for a penny a day,
Because he can't work any faster.

BOYS AND GIRLS COME OUT TO PLAY!

Boys and girls come out to play,
The moon does shine as bright as day.
Leave your supper and leave your sleep,
And join your friends out in the street.
Come with a whoop and come with a call,
Come with good will or not at all.
Up the ladder and down the wall,
A half-penny loaf will serve us all;
You find milk and I'll find flour,
And we'll have a pudding in half-an-hour.

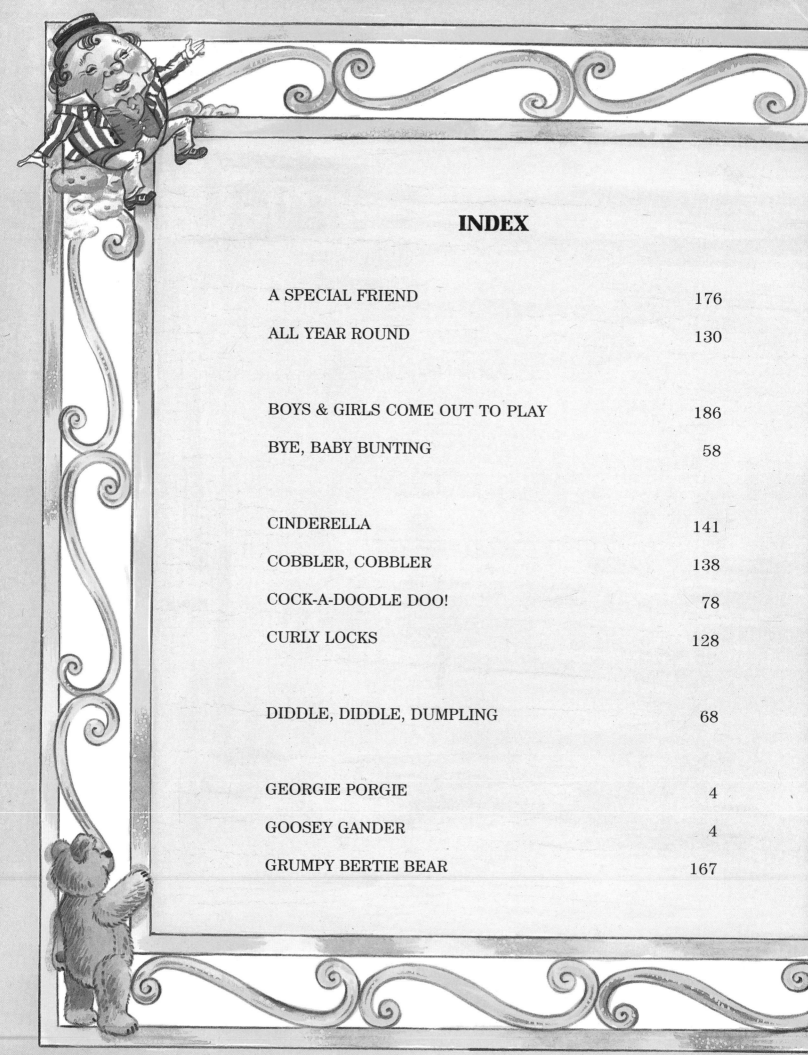

INDEX

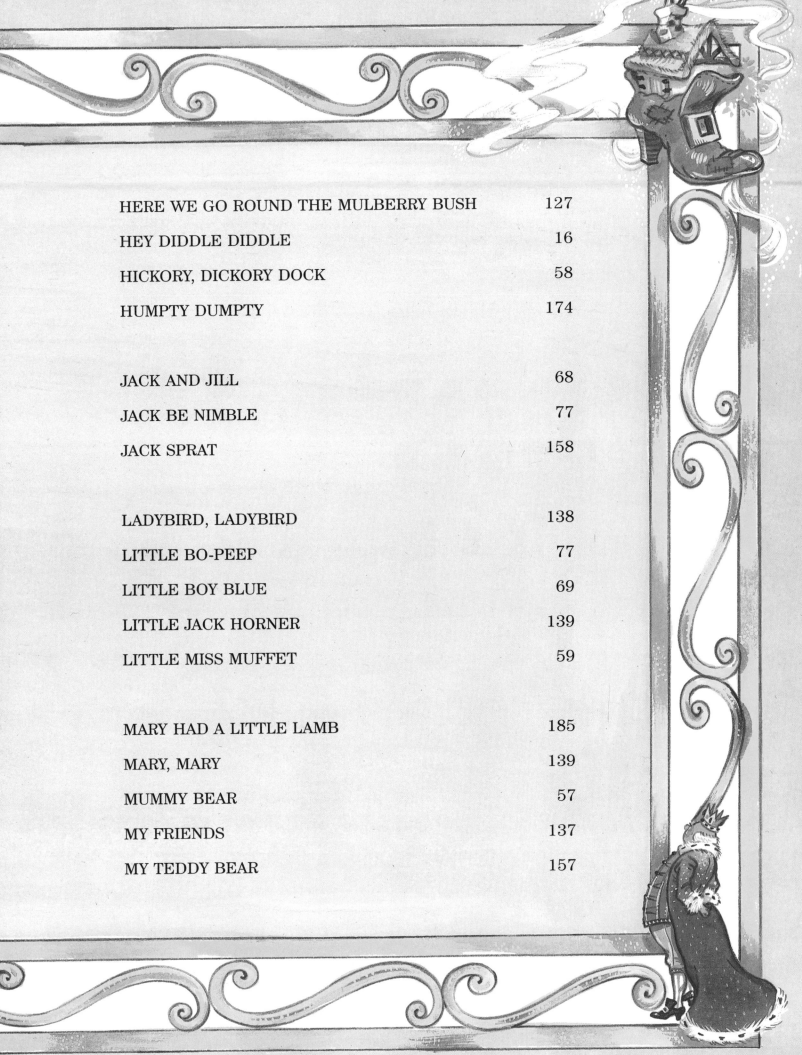

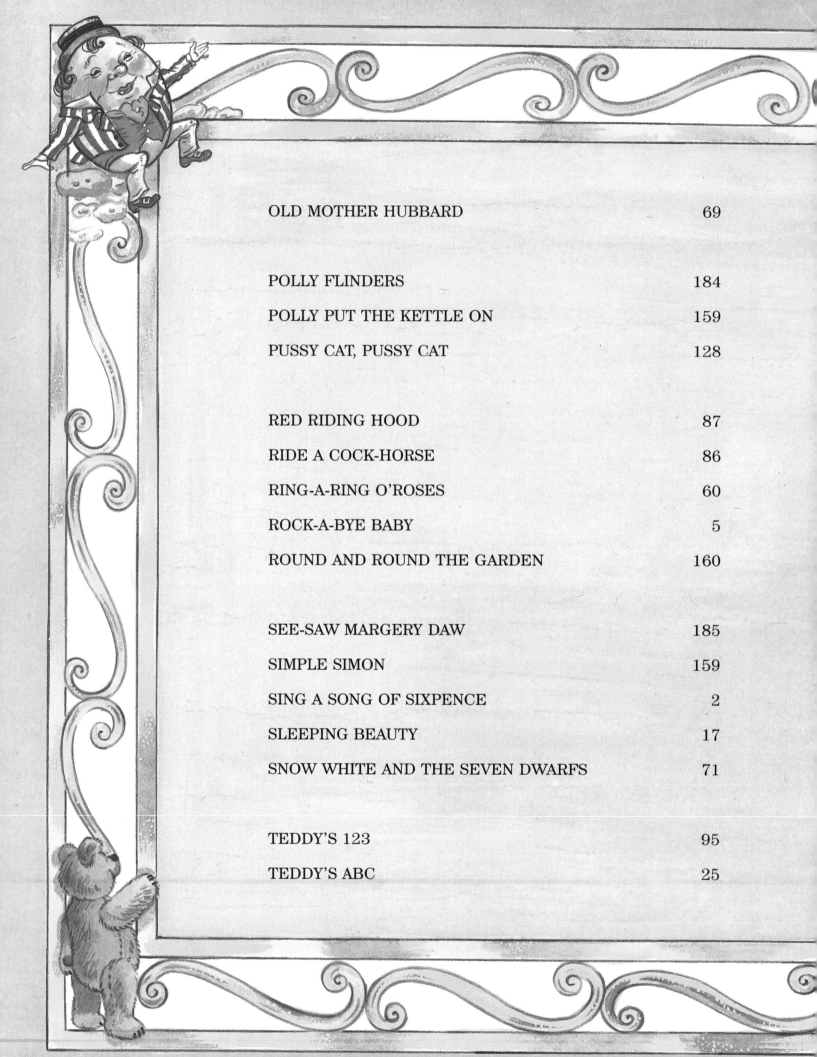

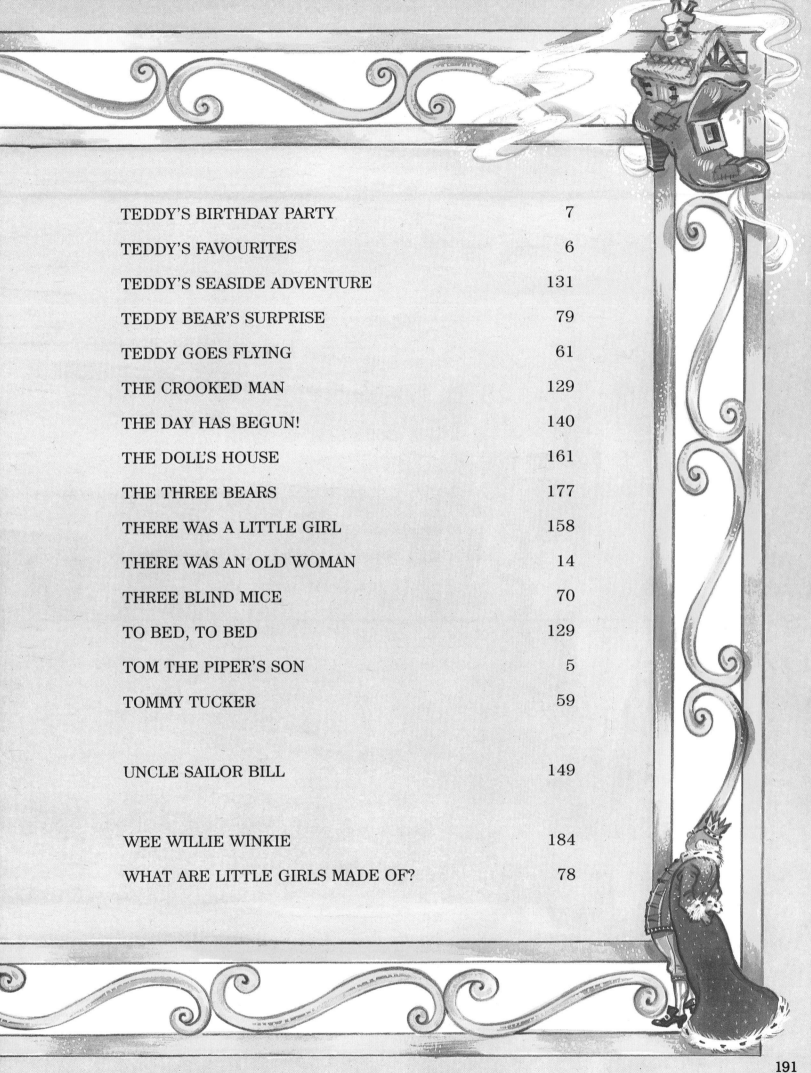

This omnibus edition first published in 2000 by Brown Watson
The Old Mill, 76 Fleckney Road,
Kibworth Beauchamp,
Leicestershire LE8 OHG